$15.96

12/4/04

P9-AQE-762

Leo's Tree

by Debora Pearson
art by Nora Hilb

Annick Press

Toronto * New York * Vancouver

When Leo was small

His father planted a tree
A scratchy branchy linden tree

This is Leo

This is his tree

Grow, little Leo
Grow, little tree

Bright warm sun
Smell of mud

Leo grows hair

Tree sprouts buds

Bumblebees nuzzle flowers
Birds flip-flap and whirl

Leo laughs, Leo waves
Hello great green world

Rosy cheeks, rosy trees
Crunchy golden linden leaves

Leo creeping

Crawling, standing ...

Leaves and Leo
All fall down!

Cat tracks
Bird tracks
Big baby boot tracks

Cozy Leo
Snowy tree
Blow wind blow

Snow is deep
Go to sleep
Dream and then ...

World wakes up
It's spring again

Seasons come
Seasons go

Slowly, slowly
Small things grow ...

Bigger Leo
Taller tree
Look! Here comes
Leo's family

This is Leo's sister

This is her tree

Grow, little Sophie
Grow, Sophie's tree

© 2004 Debora Pearson (text)
© 2004 Nora Hilb (illustrations)
Design: Sheryl Shapiro

Annick Press Ltd.

We acknowledge the support of the Canada Council for the Arts, the Ontario Arts Council, the Government of Ontario through the Ontario Book Publishers Tax Credit program and the Ontario Book Initiative, and the Government of Canada through the Book Publishing Industry Development Program (BPIDP) for our publishing activities.

The right of Debora Pearson to be identified as the Author of this Work has been asserted by her.

Cataloging in Publication

Pearson, Debora
    Leo's tree / Debora Pearson ; art by Nora Hilb.

ISBN 1-55037-845-7 (bound).—ISBN 1-55037-844-9 (pbk.)

    1. Growth--Juvenile poetry. I. Hilb, Nora II. Title.

PS8581.E343L46 2004   jC811'.6   C2003-904894-2

The art in this book was rendered in watercolor.
The text was typeset in Galahad Regular.

Distributed in Canada by: Published in the U.S.A. by Annick Press (U.S.) Ltd.
Firefly Books Ltd.   Distributed in the U.S.A. by:
66 Leek Crescent   Firefly Books (U.S.) Inc.
Richmond Hill, ON   P.O. Box 1338
L4B 1H1   Ellicott Station
                             Buffalo, NY 14205

Printed and bound in Canada by Friesens, Altona, Manitoba.

Visit us at: www.annickpress.com

For Alex and Cyrus Spears, and their family too
—D.P.

To Claudia and Vera, my sisters
—N.H.